vicious circles

Barrytown
Station Hill

vicious circles

two fictions & «after the fact»

Maurice Blanchot

translated by Paul Auster

First Edition.

Published by Station Hill Press, Barrytown, New York 12507, with partial support from the New York State Council on the Arts and the National Endowment for the Arts.

Produced by the Open Studio Typesetting & Design Project, Barrytown, New York, founded in part by the New York State Council on the Arts and the National Endowment for the Arts.

Designed by Susan Quasha.

Library of Congress Cataloging in Publication Data

Blanchot, Maurice.
Vicious circles.

Translation of: Le ressassement éternel, and of:
Après coup.
1. Blanchot, Maurice—Translations, English.
I. Blanchot, Maurice. Après coup. English. 1985.
II. Title. III. Title: After the fact.
PQ2603.L3343A225 1985 843'.912 84-8437
ISBN 0-930794-98-2
ISBN 0-930794-97-4 (pbk.)

Manufactured in the United States of America.

vicious circles

vicious circles

the idyll

The moment he entered the city, the stranger was led to the Home. His guard said to him on the way:

"You'll hold it against me, but it's the rule. No one escapes the spectacle of happiness."

"Indeed," said the stranger. "Then what's so terrible about this Home?"

"Nothing," answered the guard, suddenly cautious, "nothing at all."

They walked through an empty garden and then rang the doorbell of a large house.

"I'm going now," the guard said to him in a low voice. "But I urge you to follow my advice: don't trust appearances."

It was a young woman who opened the door. She had round cheeks and plump hands.

"Hello," she said to him. "Don't be afraid of anything. The house is open to you."

She led him into the reception room where a young man with square shoulders and an open, smiling face stood up to greet him.

"This is my husband," the young woman said, offering him a seat. "He's good; you'll like him, everyone does."

"You'll like all of us, of course," the young man added jovially. Then, looking him over and noticing his muddy clothes and dirty face: "May I ask where you come from?"

The stranger felt a lump in his throat and did not manage to give an answer.

"Later," said the young woman, "you'll tell us everything later."

She led him out of the room and up to the next floor, to a place with a vast row of showers. She handed him a comb, a brush, and a bar of soap.

"See you later," she said, giving him a little push, and then, confidingly: "wash well; we're very concerned about hygiene here."

But as soon as she had closed the door, the stranger felt his exhaustion and cried out: "I'm hungry." He sat down on the floor, and as the steaming water began to splash out from the ten nozzles on the ceiling, he was overcome with nausea and lost consciousness. He woke up on a bed. There was an orderly beside him, rubbing his face with a damp cloth.

"Take it easy," he said, nursing him amiably. "It's not a crime to be hungry."

But the stranger looked at him intensely and asked if he would soon be returned to community life.

"Community life?" asked the orderly. "Everyone lives all together here, but there's no community life."

"No," the stranger murmured, "I'm talking about a free life."

As he got up, he saw the young woman by the door, looking at him in a friendly way.

"Oh well," she said, "you can bathe another time. As soon as you can walk, come to the cafeteria. I'll be waiting for you there."

The orderly helped him slip on his miserable sandals. Then he put the stranger's clothes in order, slicked down his hair, and removed some of the mud that was splattered on his suit. Just as he opened the door, he said in his ear:

"It would be better if you went to see your comrades first."

There were about twenty of them gathered in a shed, yawning, playing cards, and drinking.

"This is the newcomer," said the orderly, speaking more or less to everyone, but most directly to a rather old man who was lying on a pile of sacks. "They're waiting for him at the cafeteria. You'll get to know him in a little while."

The young woman served the meal herself, her eyes bright, her face shining, hovering around the stranger as he ate. But after he was finished, she took his hand and asked him: "What do you think of my husband?" The stranger was shocked by this question.

"Why ask me?" he said, trying to get away. "I'm only a vagabond. I don't have time to observe people."

He imagined that he knew the words she was burning to hear.

"Oh!" she said, squeezing him harder, "just wait a few days, and then you'll come to me to talk about him. Look at me one last time."

She had the most joyful face he had ever seen.

"Well, see you soon, Alexander Akim."

This strange name suited him as well as any other: he was no more than a kind of beggar here. Once back in the shed, he lay down on the ground. They were playing and singing around him. But he could not free himself from the memory of that face.

"Where are you from?" asked the old man, crouching down beside him.

"So, you're a spy, too," he answered unpleasantly. "What difference does it make what country I come from? I'm a stranger, that's all."

The old man looked at him with a resigned and tranquil expression.

"I was born in the neighboring region," he said, "in Samard. When you cross the bridge, you can see it near a small stand of chestnut trees, and if you climb the hill, you can even make out the river that flows through the area. I have ten brothers over there, and three of them have daughters ready to be married. If you like, you can meet them later."

"Thank you," said Alexander Akim, "I already have a wife."

His bad humor did not discourage the old man, who called to one of the men yawning on the floor.

"Isaiah Sirotk, come play with us."

The cards were shuffled, cut, and dealt out, but the stranger refused to take part in the game, and all the normal cheating took place as he looked on with disapproval.

"Listen," said the old man, breaking off from the cards, "as you can see, I'm the oldest one here. All passions have died out in a man my age. In a few days, I'll be leaving the Home and returning to my country, and I'll soon forget this horrible past. Trust me, then, and if something is troubling you, confide in me."

The stranger thanked him but said there was nothing troubling him and that he only wanted to sleep. So he was left in a corner, looking with heavy eyes at these rough, slovenly men in the light of a weak electric lamp. Eventually, he managed to fall into a deep sleep. When he woke up in the morning, he was expecting to be beaten with sticks, for that was the punishment he believed was doled out to strangers. But he was led to the director, who greeted him very cordially.

"Alexander Akim," he said, after inviting him to sit down beside him on a couch, "I'm not going to question you by the rules, I'm too young to stick to protocol. Where are you from? Why have you left your country? Have you stolen anything on the way? I'm sure these questions have their usefulness, but they don't happen to interest me. My thoughts are elsewhere. My family absorbs me too much." He mused for several moments over his words, and then, gently sliding his hand along

Akim's arm, he asked softly: "Are you married? At a time when you're already beginning to worry about middle age, do you know what it means to find a young woman who has more life and freshness than all the others, a person who understands you totally, who never stops thinking about you, someone who looks for you, someone you look for yourself and who is right there beside you all the time? Have you experienced this? Do you have any idea of the upheaval this causes in your life? It drives you crazy."

He shuddered as he stood up and walked from one end of the room to the other, obviously distraught. Then he recovered his composure, took a photograph album from the table, and leafed through it calmly with his guest. These were snapshots that had been taken during his engagement. The pictures were conventional, but it was impossible not to feel the extraordinary impact created by these two radiant figures who were always turned toward each other, as though they were but two sides of a single face. This display finally irritated Alexander Akim, whose eyes no longer dared to look at the signs of such collusion. He was relieved when the director finally put an end to their meeting by saying:

"We welcome you. I hope you'll have nothing to complain about during your stay."

Right after that, he was led to the quarry to work with the other men. They were supervised by a giant, a very ugly but good-natured person who was always agitated and upset. The work consisted of taking the stones that were dug out of the mountain each day by the city laborers and carting them to a huge pit. In the heat of the sun this was an exhausting task, exhausting and useless. Why throw the stones into this pit when special trucks would be coming afterwards to haul them away? Couldn't these trucks have been loaded right after the stones were dug up, when they were sitting there in neat piles? But the vagabonds had to be given work, and vagabond work was never to any great purpose. Alexander Akim attached himself to the overseer, who secretly passed on brandy and canned goods to him. They did not go back to the Home at night; a cave hollowed out in the mountain served as their shelter, and they rested, slept, and ate there. There was hardly any comraderie among the members of this small society. Brawls sometimes broke out; but these moments of violence did not last very long and would give way to a reserve mixed with coarse behavior. It was not against the rules to exchange a few words with the laborers from the city, who were dressed in grey and green striped clothes and worked at the bottom of the hills. These were generally good-looking men, sober and serious, and they only talked to the beggarly riff-raff to reproach them for their intemperence and laziness. One of them arranged a meeting with Alexander Akim one day in the tall grass where they spent the noon hour, and without even looking at him declared that when you broke the law you should be deprived of food and lodging and should not be allowed to live comfortably in one of the most beautiful buildings in the city. The stranger left without answering him, but later he was sorry he had not clobbered this arbiter of morality. The overseer helped him to understand what was required of him. There were no major obligations: a little discipline was demanded, but only on certain days (for example, walking in single file and not talking during work). With the old man not there, the others paid no attention to the newcomer, and he likewise shunned their company. Everything was so arid in this region, with the sun burning all day long and the nights ravaged by silence and cold, that the presence of other men was seen as if through a dream. At dawn, they had to go down through a mine shaft to a little sandy beach where there was a spring. Drinking was the only thing that interested the prisoners. During the rest of the day, they would pass an alcohol-soaked rag over their lips, and the most favored ones would drink a few drops—which burned them but gave them the illusion of a new life. After a week, Akim went back to the Home. Just as he was leaving, the overseer said to him:

"I was married once, too. But women don't like my job. People who live with vagabonds aren't liked."

Covered with dust, his face dried out, his hands torn, Akim was sent to the infirmary where he became seriously ill, in spite of the good treatment he received. Every afternoon, when the memory of the sun became strongest, he would feel as though he were entering a false night; instead of bringing him sleep and coolness, it was all flames and storms. They wrapped him in icy sheets, but to no avail; his body was burning him and he would call out for the water that had refreshed him earlier, yet he would never drink it. The director came to see him.

"What's wrong with you?" he asked. "Why this sudden indisposition? Everyone else always feels so well here. Are you subject to these kinds of attacks?"

The sick man gave him a hateful look.

"You've treated me brutally," he said in a low voice. "A dog, a swine has the right to more respect. I'll remember your hospitality."

"What's that?" murmured the director, startled by so much passion. "Your words disappoint me. I've done everything I can to make things easy for you. Have you been slighted somehow?"

"Yes, as a matter of fact, I've been slighted," he cried out, totally beside himself with anger, and then, forgetting where he was, he started to scream: "Get out, get out," so that the director left without saying another word.

He was put in a dark cell where he continued to receive the best care. Only a feeble light came through the air vent, and he felt as though he had been cut off from the world forever, so great was the silence. The orderly tried to encourage him.

"Naturally," he said, "it's hard to have your freedom taken away from you. But is anyone ever free? Can we do what we want? And there are so many other reasons for being unhappy."

"Thank you," said Akim, "but you won't console me with the thought of others' unhappiness. My suffering belongs to me."

The fever let up, and the stranger abandoned hope of leaving his prison through a dream that would be more lasting than his nightmares.

"When can I leave this cell?" he asked. "Have I done such a terrible thing? You're not responsible for what you do in a delirium."

The orderly went to find out.

"I couldn't find the director," he said when he returned. And then he added with an air of irritation: "The atmosphere is stormy."

Nevertheless, he was finally let out, and Akim went back to his comrades. He was surprised by the animation that reigned among them, and even though calm returned as soon as they saw him, he noticed a kind of satisfaction or unpleasant interest on their faces.

"What is it now?" he asked peevishly. "What are you hiding from me?"

"Be quiet," the old man said to him. "It's not your job to tell us what we can and can't do. Everyone here has his own prison, but in that prison each person is free."

One of the men, the one called Isaiah Sirotk, insulted him crudely. "Spy," he shouted at him, "informer." The two men began to scuffle. Akim let himself be taken by the throat. He saw his adversary's face, the large protruding ears, the eyes without irises, the hideous features. The old man separated them and swore loudly, but he suddenly stopped talking because a manservant stuck his head through the window and invited the stranger to go to the director.

"Listen," the old man said, pushing him into a corner, "you've already noticed that the director and his wife hate each other. It's a silent hatred with no cause, a terrible feeling that disrupts the whole house. It doesn't even have to be violent to be felt. Calm and hypocrisy are enough. Still, sometimes there are scenes. You can hear the shouting through the walls. It's better to be shut up in a cell than to appear before them."

"Is that so?" said the stranger. "You're so spiteful that now you're trying to upset me with lies just when I need my composure. Why are you trying to ruin me? What have I done?"

He was taken into the large reception room where he had been the first day. There were flowers scattered over the floor. Others had been made into garlands on the table.

"Well, what is it?" the director asked him, his face pinched and apparently unwell. "I only have a little time."

"May I see your wife?" the stranger asked, after giving him a furtive look.

"Yes, yes, of course," the director answered with a distracted smile. "But today is her birthday, and it would be better to wait a little."

The stranger apologized and then remained silent.

"Is that all?" the director asked impatiently. "Don't you have any other questions to ask me? Tell me why you've bothered me like this."

"But I'm only here because you sent for me," the stranger said.

"That's true," said the director with confusion. "Forgive me. I'm feeling out of sorts. I'd like to offer my apologies for the punishment you were given. It was painful for me to behave like that towards a sick man. Try to forget it—and come back to see me."

Akim was about to leave, but the director held him back,

saying, "I'll go call Louise. She'll be happy to say a few words to you." They came back together, she leaning on his arm, he bending towards her. Akim was struck by the youthfulness that lit up their features when they were together. The director seemed completely recovered. He was smiling and moving impishly with small steps.

"Stay and have a drink with us," she said to him, extending her hand. "Did Pierre tell you it's my birthday?" Then, on the way out: "Come back tomorrow, we'll talk."

When he returned to the shed he lay down, determined to stay apart from his comrades. But they all gathered around him, and he had to hold his own against them, contradicting everything they said in a sharp voice.

"Get out of here," the old man shouted, dispersing the group. Then he crouched down in his usual way. "Forgive me, Alexander Akim. You've been sick. You've been separated from the others. I should have been a better companion. Are you willing to listen to me today?"

"Let me sleep."

"Yes, you're going to sleep. But listen to me first. I don't want to be a nuisance. This is a request, a very humble prayer. Maybe you think I'm trying to slander the director?"

"To hell with your thoughts! I'm sick, I need to be alone."

"That's it, you think I have something against him. But no, he's a good man. He's always been generous with me. He could have sent me away, and yet he keeps me on, old as I am. Is he responsible for his unhappiness? Is there anything shameful in being unhappy? And what unhappiness could be more terrible than hating instead of loving yourself?"

"Enough of this, or I'll call the overseer."

'One more word. In your opinion, which one of them is to blame? She's a loose woman, a spoiled child; but he's so somber, so severe, how can anyone live with him?"

Seeing that the stranger had turned over on his side and was no longer listening, he withdrew with a sigh. The next morning, Akim went to the infirmary, where the young woman was treating several indigent men from the city. She made a friendly sign to him but didn't say anything. He went on wandering about the halls of the Home, searching through the empty rooms for traces of a drama that continued to elude him. That day the whole house was open to him. He walked into the administrative offices where, among the files and shelves loaded with documents, there was a flower in a frame, a touching and useless object that stirred up the memory of a faultless love. He lingered beside half-closed drawers, as if the letters he dared not read were meant to prove to him that an affection still existed. He entered the director's apartment. The walls were bare; shells, engraved stones, and glasses tinted with friendly colors adorned the mantlepiece and furniture. It seemed as though a wild river had flowed through these rooms, leaving behind the debris of earth and uprooted weeds in images of glass. Green branches went up to the ceiling, and it was impossible to say if this profusion would wither by the next day or if the garden on the floor would soon be giving off flowers and new leaves. Before he had discovered how this juvenile ornamentation was put together, Akim was surprised by the return of Louise. She looked at him dreamily for several moments.

"My room is around the hall," she said. "But let's stay here."

They sat down ceremoniously—he on a chair, she on a bench.

"You really are a stranger," she remarked. "Perhaps you'll begin to fit in to the way we live and work here, but I'd be surprised if you ever forgot your country."

Akim didn't answer.

"What do you find so displeasing about your city? Its size? Its overly tall houses? Its narrow streets? Are you put off by the Home? Have you left someone behind that you miss? I'd like to help you."

"You can," said Akim, straightening up. A new and unexpected expression transformed his face. "I'm suffering because I'm not free. Let me become the man I was before."

"But that's easy," said the young woman. "Your quarantine is almost over. Tomorrow you can visit the city if you like and talk to the people who live there." Then she added: "I'd like to tell you my story."

He listened as she spoke in that childish but cold voice of hers. Predictably, it was the story of her engagement.

"I don't understand why you confide in me like this," he interrupted her. "I know you're happy, even though people say the opposite, but in my situation I can't get mixed up in the private lives of people who are above me."

He thanked her and went back to his comrades. His first walk through the city did not make much of an impression on him. The houses were majestic, but the streets were narrow and irregular, and they lacked air. He was recognized by his slow, provincial way of walking. Entering a bookstore, he was questioned good-naturedly by the owner.

"Are you satisfied with your stay at the Home? What luxury there, what comfort! The people of the city are happy to have it, since it allows them to welcome strangers in the best possible way. We don't like people to live in exile among us."

Akim listened with an air of irritation.

"And what a good director!" said the bookstore owner. "He's an educated and just man. His troubles only make you like him more."

"Thank you for your kindness," Akim said. "Do you happen to have a detailed map of the city and the surrounding area?"

"A map of the city, yes. But we're not very interested in other regions. On the other hand, here is an excellent book about the Home."

The work was illustrated with photographs and, as he expected, it was filled with praise for the penal methods that were such a source of pride to the State: the mixture of severity and gentleness, the combination of freedom and restraint—these were the fruit of long experience, and it was difficult to imagine a more just or reasonable system. When he returned to the Home, he found the director sprawled out on a bench in the garden, his face livid.

"Are you in pain?" he asked. "Do you want me to call for help?"

"Mind your own business," the director answered. "It's only a passing attack; I'd rather be alone."

The house was plunged in silence. Decorated with those wild flowers that are little more than colored grass, it seemed more than ever to be the place of a simple and happy dream.

"A sad house," the orderly said to him, walking in a distracted way through the halls, far from the room where he was supposed to be working. "How can two young people go at each other like that? Who's pushing them to torment each other? The only time they're not in silent despair is when they burst out in anger at each other. And that constant trembling, the suffering in their mouths, their eyes, their hands, whenever they have to see or touch each other."

In the shed, the overseer was whipping a young prisoner—the unfortunate Nicholas Pavlon. Overcome by a burning fever, he had walked through the city almost naked. Akim saw how inhuman the ordeal of flogging was. At the tenth stroke, the victim fainted; the torturer, exhausted by his own violence, began to shudder, as though some poison had suddenly chilled his blood. The old man said to Akim:

"Tomorrow my detention is over. But I've come to an age when you stop hoping for a new life. What illusions could I have after all this useless suffering? Can I still get married? Do I still have enough faith to join myself to a woman and live in peace? No. Everything is finished for a man who gets out of prison."

"Why are you complaining today?" asked Akim. "Yesterday you were thanking the director for not getting rid of you because of your age. Is living in the Home a privilege or a curse?"

The old man made no response. He turned and gave some advice to the prisoners who were sprinkling water on the body of the unfortunate young man.

"If he doesn't wake up before sunset, he'll be lost," he said.

He didn't wake up. The blood had stopped flowing from his body, and the men covered him with the long blanket he had used to wrap himself in at night. Even though Akim had no real feeling for this naive and rough companion, he felt as though his heart had been torn apart, and he let the old man spend the evening with him—groaning, complaining, and rambling on.

"What makes them enemies?" he said. "The lack of family? Orphans can never find happiness. They don't have the gentle common instinct that lies at the heart of family life to prepare them for living with others. And they themselves have no child. They hate everything that could make life easier for them.

"They've made a fatal mistake," he went on. "They thought love was drawing them together, but they really detested each other. Certain signs led them to think they were tied to the same destiny, but it was really a desire to tear each other apart through disagreements and torments. How long did they fool themselves? When they finally discovered the marks of their old intimacy on their bodies, it was too late; these marks did no more than prove to them the fury that has been holding them together. They must go on loving each other in order to go on hating each other.

"Has she deceived him?" he said. "No, she's been very careful; she's denied him the possibility of moving away from her a little, of breathing some other air, another life perhaps free of violent feelings. She doesn't leave him, and in that way she can overwhelm him with her solicitude. This makes him see all the hatred she has for him, all the detachment she inspires in him. She follows him around, as if her only reason for existing were to represent the void his life has become. He's calmer than she is. But nothing ever distracts him from his despair. He's silent. He speaks without caring what he says. When he says nothing, his silence is made into something infinitely sad, humiliated, contemptible. Unhappy young people. Sad house."

"Shut up," said Akim, losing all patience as these disjointed words went on and on. But as he shook the old man, he saw that his eyes were empty and inflamed, just as they were whenever he drank the water with alcohol in it. He tucked him in roughly and then passed the night in the calm that surrounds the dead.

Nicholas Pavlon was given a magnificent funeral. A bier with innumerable flowers stacked around it was set out in the largest room of the Home. The men took turns watching over it, and the overseer, the unwilling instrument of misery, did not leave the dead man, sitting behind the momument in a low chair, sinking into a deep regret over his terrible violence. The procession passed slowly through the city. The stranger had time to study the tall buildings that seemed to merge together in the sky, the dark and narrow shops, the apartments that became more elegant and spacious once they reached the upper floors. He was told that the cemetery was located in the center of the city; it stretched up the side of a hill in a swampy region surrounded by walls that marked off an enclosure. The solemnity of the ceremony, the apparent sadness of the city dwellers weeping falsely for a dead stranger, and the crudeness of the prisoners dressed up in party clothes, inspired a disgust in Akim that would have made him leave the procession immediately if he had not been afraid of being punished. At the moment when the director threw some flowers on the coffin, which had been set beside the grave, and spoke some words befitting the occasion, Akim could not stop himself from shouting out: "What's going on here? Is this a farce, a mockery—the revenge of depraved men?" But he regretted these words, since the people around him thought he was overcome with grief. Still, he could not have done otherwise. Back at the Home, he had to attend another ceremony: the old man's departure. All the prisoners were gathered in the reception room, still warm with the smell of death. Flowers, no less brilliant than the ones on the bier, transformed this farewell ceremony into something that felt like an engagement party. The old man, filled with emotion and already drunk, believed that he had committed grave injustices against those who were there, asked forgiveness, kept walking around the chairs and tables.

'You have honored this institution," the director said, smiling. "You're going home completely adjusted. I'm sure your stay here has not always been agreeable; there are dark hours when everything becomes inexplicable, when you blame the ones who love you, when the punishments seem to be absurd cruelties. But in every life it is so. The essential thing is to leave prison one day."

Everyone applauded. Akim wanted to ask something, but he was ashamed to speak up in front of all these people, and he withdrew silently into a corner. After the reception, the director called for him:

"I sense that you're impatient, troubled. That's not good. It will make getting used to your new life even harder. In my opinion, you're wrong not to see things as they are: you're in a house where we have your best interests in mind; you should leave it to us and not worry about unpleasant things."

The director was standing beside the table. His wife was sitting behind him, and she smiled as she listened. "Is it possible that they hate each other?" Akim asked himself. "No, everything is a travesty in this city. They love each other. At the most, they have the usual quarrels of young married people."

"I'm not troubled," he answered. "I don't understand the customs of the house and I suffer from it, that's all. If I'm allowed to go back to my own country, I'll always remember your excellent hospitality."

"He's a stranger," Louise said joyfully. "I always thought so—he'll never really fit in here."

"How long are you going to keep me prisoner?" he asked.

"Prisoner?" answered the director, frowning. "Why do you say prisoner? The Home isn't a jail. You weren't allowed to go out for several days for reasons of hygiene, but now you're free to go wherever you like in the city."

"Excuse me," said Akim, "I meant to say: when can I leave the Home?"

"Later," said the director, annoyed, "later. And besides, Alexander Akim, that depends on you. When you no longer feel like a stranger, then there will be no problem in becoming a stranger again."

He laughed. Akim wanted to get back at him for this joke, but he was overcome by sadness.

"You wife explained it: I'll never be anything but a man from another city."

"Please, please, no discouragement. My wife says anything that pops into her head; you mustn't take it seriously."

He leaned over Louise and caressed her shoulders. Akim looked at them for a moment before returning to the shed.

The vagabonds, who had secretly carried off some provisions, were still carousing. They were drinking and singing sad songs of this sort:

Land of my birth,
Why did I leave you?

I've lost my youth
And live with woe.
Loveless now
And jailed forever,
Death alone is not my foe.

They greeted Akim warmly, but soon Isaiah and a prisoner named Gregory began quarrelling. One was reproaching the other for having borrowed money from him.

"Give me back my money," Gregory was saying. "I'm not angry that you took it from me, but today I need it. Come on, give it back to me."

"Shut up, you souse," Isaiah answered. "Where would you earn any money? You stole it, that's what you did."

"Stole it?" said Gregory, suddenly overwhelmed by the enormity of the accusation. "Stole it? If anyone's a thief, it's you. I earned that money by working. It's my money from my work."

"Listen," said Isaiah impatiently. "You're drunk and you talk too much. There's no salary here. If you really earned that money, it's because you were paid to spy on us. I'll teach you what happens to stool pigeons." And he jumped at his throat.

These accusations of spying were frequent, and perhaps they were justified. After all, why not betray men you did not like? There was no sense of teamwork, each man lived for himself, and it was even taken for granted that the heterogeneity of the group would give rise to secret enmities. The absence of the old man weighed heavily on Akim. The old man had been the only person he could talk to. That evening, he felt that he had to talk to someone; he would die of suffocation if he could not get out of his thoughts. The memory of the director and his wife tormented him so cruelly that he felt drunk, drunk with a passion whose true nature no one else could see. He detested them, since they were responsible for his exile; and yet a feeling of tenderness touched him whenever he thought about them, this charming couple who lived in the simplicity of the heart. Yes, sometimes he wished that despair would tear them apart, that they would be dragged through endless torments, that hatred would be the sole bond between them. For what else was waiting for him in the world but hatred and torment? And yet, can you close your eyes to the truth? It was enough for him to recall those two handsome faces, the looks they exchanged, the naturalness of their smiles, to feel that bitter peace that comes when the spectacle of happiness is too close to you. He tried to rouse the overseer. The man was sleeping, exhausted by the day's emotions.

"Why all these lies about the director?" he shouted at him.

Torn from the consolation of sleep—and plunged back into the remorse that would not stop tormenting him—the giant groaned and then uttered a string of irrational words.

"I'm not a donkey that can be woken up any which way. I need sleep. Just leave me alone."

Akim shook him a second time.

"Let me take a walk around the house. There's no air in here, I'm suffocating."

The overseer swore and covered his face with his arms.

"Have the good sense to let me go out," Akim said a last time.

He kicked the sleeping man in the ribs with his boots. The man rose slowly, distraught, his eyes expressionless; then he staggered, as if trying to find a middle path between sleeping and waking; suddenly, a look of anguish came over his face; Akim did not have time to get out of the way, and he saw the man grimace and begin to vomit. Outside, the wind shook the trees, and the dry noise of the leaves rubbing against each other reminded him of an arid stretch of sand. A bitter smell came in gusts, now exciting and agreeable, now fetid; the swamps turned the night into a kind of trap, and it was unwise to get caught in it. The stranger sat on the bench and imagined having a conversation with the overseer.

"Lies?" said the guard. "I've known about them too long to want to talk about them. Leave these stories alone."

"Ah," said Akim, "that's just what I need: someone who's known about them for a long time. This isn't like other stories, is it?"

"In any case, it's not a story to analyze and repeat. Is it important to you?"

"No, no, not at all," said Akim. "But answer my question: are they happy or unhappy?"

The overseer sniffed, and the stranger did not dare to repeat his question. He said:

"Have they been married long?"

"Two years."

"And when they were married, they acted the same as they do today?"

"Yes."

"You see," said Akim, "if nothing has changed, it means that they've always been happy. Happiness is not deceptive. I'm sure they're bound together by a great and profound attachment."

The overseer continued to sniff.

"Is that your opinion?"

"Don't ask for my opinion on this subject. I'm an overseer. I don't know anything except what I see."

"Precisely. Tell me what you've seen." Silence from the guard. "Well," said Akim, "you're afraid to talk. I'll find out everything myself."

"No, Alexander Akim, don't try to find out: what good will it do? I'm going to speak to you with an open heart. I would tell this to anyone. When they were married, I already had my job at the Home. I had a wife, too. For the first few days, they didn't leave their room. There was a strange silence in the house, a feeling of idleness. In spite of all the work, you didn't know what to do with yourself. After a week, some strangers came, and I had to go tell them. In the first room, I didn't find anyone. There was dust on the furniture, as if no one had lived there for several years. I was afraid, I called out. Then, I went into the little office. But no one was there either. Everything was in order, and yet I already knew that something dreadful had happened. I stood there for several moments waiting. I wanted to run away. I thought they were both dead. But finally I opened the door a crack and lifted the curtain. They were sitting apart, not looking at each other, not looking at anything at all. I couldn't read anything in their faces. The only thing was that air of emptiness, and it made me turn away. Yes, an air that explained this bleak, heavy silence that was indifferent to misery, without bitterness towards anyone. I felt that I couldn't stay there. I moved, and he looked at me and said: 'Yes, yes, I'm coming.' "

"Is that all?" asked Akim. "But what you're describing is tranquil happiness, something extraordinary—the feeling that's at the heart of every idyll, a true happiness without words."

"Really?" said the overseer. "Really? Is that what you would call it?"

The stranger again heard the noise of the leaves, and they made the wind seem dry and barren. The smell became suffocating. Around the house, a ditch was forming where all the swampy odors of the city were stagnating. He returned and found the overseer sleeping soundly on a pile of sacks. But the next morning the man told him viciously:

"No going out at night. You'll get five lashes for that."

Towards the beginning of the afternoon, just when he was planning to go to the city, the old man arrived with the members of his family: two young men with brown skin who said nothing, and three girls, all of them small and fat. The old man said to his comrades: "These are my brothers' children," and he introduced Akim to the youngest girl. She was wearing a white cotton dress. The girls, who were at first intimidated, got it into their heads to tour the famous establishment, which was off limits to the families of prisoners before the prisoners were released. They ran idiotically through the halls, into the rooms on the first floor where the showers were located, and down into the dark cells, which had been dug out beneath the cellar.

"I didn't recognize anyone in the village," the old man said. "I feel out of place among my own people. The memory of the homeland can't survive the passing of time."

Akim thought these words were meant to console him, but they pointlessly wounded his hope.

"I got a friendly welcome. But what does it matter if kindness comes from people who are no more than strangers? I'm too old."

The girls came back, out of breath, their eyes sparkling, their faces shining with sweat. They were ugly but agreeable.

"I'll be back," the old man said to Akim. "Look to the future."

Even though he had only a short time to visit the city, once again he plunged into the narrow streets and stopped in to see the bookseller.

"You really don't have any works on the surrounding countries?" he asked. "No postcards, no pictures?"

"I'd be surprised if I did," said the bookseller. "But I'll go look if it will make you happy."

As he climbed the ladder and rapidly threw the books he chose from the shelves into his apron, Akim asked him:

"Is it true that the director and his wife..."

"Is what true?" said the bookseller.

"Aren't they happy?"

"If you don't know, who would?" said the bookseller. "The prisoners are always very well informed. We learn many things from them."

"Well, I believe their marriage has been a true idyll. I've

rarely seen such a perfect relationship."

"Well, well," said the bookseller, climbing down. "I think I've found what you want."

It was a very old book that gave the history of the entire region and even included a few pictures. Akim asked if there weren't any more recent works.

"This is very rare," said the bookseller, not understanding. "You can study it at your leisure, but I can't allow you to take it away. You can consult it at this desk."

Akim sat down on a high stool. Enjoying the calm that reigned in the shop, he learned more than he had expected from his reading.

"Louise was my pupil," the bookseller suddenly said. "She often played in this store, and she learned to read from my books."

"Right here?" asked Akim.

"Yes, here. She was a very lively child, but well-behaved. Pictures and beautifully engraved letters enchanted her. She was very good at imitating their shapes. Who wouldn't have wished to see her happy?"

"Look who's curious," said Akim. Then, after studying some of the illustrations, he asked if he might not also be able to copy the most beautiful parts. Permission was given to him, but as it was growing late, he abruptly left the store.

At the Home, a work party was waiting for him. A group of unpleasant looking men, haggard and exhausted, had been collected in the street and were now shut up in the enclosure that served as a courtyard for the prisoners. The strangers who had been in the house for a while had to take turns looking after the new arrivals—to make it easier for them to bear the anxieties of this unwonted seclusion. Akim said to one of these miserable creatures:

"You'll learn that in this house it's hard to be a stranger.

You'll also learn that it's not easy to stop being one. If you miss your country, every day you'll find more reasons to miss it. But if you manage to forget it and begin to love your new place, you'll be sent home, and then, uprooted once more, you'll begin a new exile."

These words were reported to the director, who made it known to Akim that he would be punished if this happened again. Akim immediately asked for an audience. His request was turned down. The next day, he had to go to the quarries with the newcomers, even though he had been led to believe that he would never be exposed to such an ordeal again—because of his illness, because of everything he had been told, and because of his conduct, which had been that of a free man. He found himself in a landscape burned by heat, with scrawny mountains on which precise and disciplined workers scratched like insects, surrounded by vast ditches that were filled with stones and little by little emptied by the trucks—and he was flooded with exaltation, convinced that he would either perish from this terrible isolation or find the way to freedom. Scraps of reality came to him in his delirium, but no sooner did they come than he cursed them. He ran towards one of the workers, grabbed his pick, and then banged it savagely against a rock. It seemed to him that he could find new dignity in this work, which was more useful than the vagabond's work, and each blow of the pick made him feel as though he were striking another blow against the walls of his prison. At the same time, he tasted some unknown freshness under the sun, as if, in the midst of a tormenting despair, among all the jostlings of hatred, some pure and gracious feeling had remained. But then, torn from this delirium and shut up in the cave, he fell back into a despondency that made him indifferent to the passing of time, and soon he found himself with the prisoners in one of the convoys returning to the Home. It was the old man Piotl—he was not able to use his real name—who welcomed him, along with his youngest niece. This time she was wearing a dress with bright colors and had poppies in her hair.

"I've come to see you every day," he said to him. "I have a real fondness for you, and I want to do something to help you. You could marry my niece."

Akim knew from reading the little book that a prisoner who got married could leave the Home immediately to be with his wife. But he was horrified by such a practice and flatly refused.

"There's delicacy in your refusal," Piotl said. "It only makes me admire you more. But think about my offer and you'll be able to overcome the repugnance that prevents you from accepting."

That night following his return, he heard a terrible cry that sent shudders through him. Thrusting aside the guard, he rushed towards the house, where he found Louise running through the halls in a flimsy nightgown. Her face was white, and she held her hands before her as though pushing away the darkness.

"In the name of heaven, what's wrong? What's happened?"

"He's there," she said, pointing to the door of the reception room, "and he's going to kill me."

The door opened and Pierre appeared, a coat slung over his shoulders, his face even more pale than his wife's. She let out a second cry that resounded horribly through the house; and then she fell down in a faint. Pierre went towards the stranger and then, when he was close enough to touch him: "Is it an idyll?" he asked. "Is it really an idyll?" Then he turned to his wife, carried her with Akim's help into the room, and put her in a large chair. The lights were shining in the house. It looked like a celebration, as though the clusters of light were tossing open flowers around the room. Something pure had turned the silence into a ceremony for the consecration of young souls. Akim slowly left the room, but before closing the door he nevertheless said to Pierre:

"An idyll? Yes, why not?"

The next day, he left early for the bookstore to make sketches of the pictures that had interested him. The morning air in the city was clear, as though renewed by the night; and yet at night a kind of poison came out of the earth, heavier and more loaded with stench than the deepest swamps. The bookseller greeted him jovially.

"I have a new book for you," he said. "You'll find a large map in it with many details. It's very precious."

Akim made rough sketches of the less simple routes; the others he would be able to remember.

"I'm probably going to get married," he told the bookseller, who was following his work with curiosity.

"Ah, yes! Marriage!" said the bookseller. "It's the great hope of youth. To love, to live with the person you love, to enter a new world in which you are at home both with yourself and another, of course that's the dream.

"I'm getting married in order to leave the Home," said Akim, continuing with his work.

"Good idea. If that's your destiny, I can only approve. But perhaps you shouldn't decide so hastily. The Home has its advantages. To be housed and fed, to enjoy all the modern comforts, and to give only a few rare moments of work in exchange—it's not a bad life. The rest of us envy you."

"To be free, that's what counts," said Akim, getting up and carefully sliding the documents into his pocket.

"Of course," said the bookseller. "Who doesn't wish for freedom? In this heavy and monotonous life, we look in vain for something to hope for. Everything is dark, everything is spoiled. You're right, you should get married."

On the road back, Akim bought some flowers from a young woman who ran a store in the garret of a dilapidated house: her flowers seemed beautiful to him.

"I'm getting married," he told her. "Pick some flowers for me that will last until tomorrow."

He gave her a little money (he too had caught the habit of stealing) and before returning took a long walk through the city, carefully studying the streets, questioning passers-by, acting like a man whose days as a stranger would soon be over. In the early hours of the afternoon, the moment he saw Piotl—who was becoming more and more hunched over, older even than an old man—he said to him:

"Forget what I said to you yesterday. I'll gladly marry your niece. She might not always be happy with me, since I'm often moody and find it difficult to be away from my country, but I'll behave like a loyal and faithful husband."

The two men went to the director.

"A marriage?" he said, in that attentive and indulgent voice of his that made him the brother of every unfortunate person. "This is good news, Alexander Akim. I'll tell my wife right away, and she can get to work preparing the happy day with you."

Louise was of course delighted. She would have liked to wait several days, since there were so many things to take care of.

"No," said Akim, "it will be tomorrow."

"Yes, tomorrow," said old Piotl. "At my age, you don't put off days of happiness."

This was a lot to ask, for marriage was a solemn and important ceremony, and it called for many preparations. There were flowers to attend to; lights had to be lit throughout the house; every resident of a certain status was allowed to eat with the new citizen—and to take advantage of the occasion by visiting the famous but by no means well-known institution. On top of that, the hangings had to be changed twice during the day; in the morning there would be gray and black curtains to symbolize the sadness of a man in permanent exile from his country, and in the afternoon there would be bright, multicolored drapes covered with ornaments and delicate emblems. The stranger would die in the morning, and in the afternoon an old friend would take his place. There would be a young woman on his arm, and she would be surprised by the fact that she was accompanied by a man who was no longer unknown to her. The director took Akim off to the side and said:

"Once married, you can never go back home. You have to say good-bye to the past."

"I'm ready," Akim answered.

The fiancée arrived, surrounded by her sisters and brothers, an entire family who silently observed the man who had been announced as her bridegroom several days ago. They were coarse men, their faces scarred by blows; but a naive goodness came forth from their features, and Akim already loved them as the witnesses of his own transformation—a transformation they would help him to achieve, but without understanding it, and perhaps without even noticing it. The girl told him her name.

"Elise," he said to her, moved by her simplicity, "you're at an age when you still don't understand everything, but you can feel many things that other people know nothing about. I ask you to forgive me in advance for the pains I will cause you and the misfortunes that will sadden you. Perhaps it would have been better if someone else were holding you in his arms and making you promises of happiness. Why has fate chosen you? I'm sorry, and yet I'm also happy about it, for it's a sweet thing to leave a mark on an innocent soul, even at the price of much sadness."

"Until tomorrow," he said, and he kissed her thick red fingers.

Louise sent everyone away so that she would have nothing to think about except the party. She went over the formalities with Akim, told him how he was to behave, and informed him about the language that would be used: during the entire day, the director of the Home was supposed to be like his father; he would introduce him to a new world; he would protect him and help him. Akim took note of these oddities. Then, after thanking her and telling her that she and her husband had been the only people who had helped him to live through such a long period of unhappiness, he added as he left:

"If I'm getting married, it's because I believe in your happiness. The despair, the torments you inflict on each other, the hatred you have for each other, the apologies that take so much out of you—everyone can see these things. But I can only see your love, and I think that a life in which such an idyll can blossom must be a happy one."

He returned to the shed, where he had to spend one last night. The overseer, inspired by the day's exceptional events, wanted to tell him the story of his marriage, which had made him both happy and unhappy.

"To love, to be loved," he said, "that's not enough. The circumstances also have to be favorable. Could my wife stay married to a man who lived in such a disagreeable house, living beside such an unfortunate couple? She left me, and I don't even know where she is."

The evening seemed long to Akim, sitting beside this giant who did not sleep. The other prisoners, warmed by the hope of an extraordinary day, tried to get close to the man responsible for this pleasure. Several of them also thought of marriage; weren't there families in which the children waited and waited to get married? It seemed to them that chance alone had selected Akim for this happy fate, and they too were ready to claim the same privilege.

"How noisy you are!" Akim said. "If you're punished, no party tomorrow."

But when silence and sleep came, the night was no less long, and the stranger had to go out to put an end to it. Outside, even though there were no stars or moon, he found the door and started walking down the road. The air was somewhat tainted, but soft. The sleeping city, hidden in the fog, let him pass, and he had no trouble recognizing the streets. Soon, he came to the cemetery. The wall was impregnable; the doors resisted him. Still, he had to cross this area, for he didn't know how far the swamp extended, and the only sure path was among the graves. He managed to climb over the gate and then made his way through the mounds to the road that led to the most populous neighborhood in the city. Just as he was leaving the cemetery, he felt the strange effects of the corrupted air; he was choking, but he did not experience the painful sensation that goes with asphyxia; on the contrary, he felt overcome by a lovely drunkenness. Beyond the gate, he became lucid again and slowly tried to find his way among unfamiliar streets. The map he had made that morning was fresh in his mind, but the city had changed; the houses, built one on top of the other, and made even more jumbled by the darkness, opened awkwardly onto alleyways in which people glided by. It seemed that by entering these streets he was entering the houses themselves; courtyards were mixed up with public squares; bridges went from one building to another and ran above the houses like endless balconies; as soon as you found a little open space, it meant that you were shut up in a garden, and to discover a new exit you had to climb stairs and plunge on through constructions you had no way of knowing would ever lead you outside.

After wandering hopelessly, Akim came to a vast promenade lined with great motionless trees. Perhaps this was the end of the city, perhaps this was the beginning of a new life, but as he was crushed by fatigue, he fell down and almost immediately a guard led him back to the Home. Again numbed by fever, he appeared before the director, who acted in the role of judge.

"You are guilty of a disturbing act," he said sadly. "You have deceived a girl by proposing marriage to her, when all along you were only thinking about running away. You have deceived us by causing us to relax our surveillance—under the pretext of preparing this wedding. You have upset the order of the house. Do you see any way to escape punishment?"

Akim wanted only to listen without interrupting.

"Punishments are rare," the director went on, "but they are necessary. I don't know how justice works in your country; each place is different, and it's not easy to imagine someone else's customs. But whatever the difference might be from people to people, the guilty can never be spared, nor can great crimes call for anything but great punishments. Do you accept this principle?"

"I await your judgment."

"My judgment is based on what you did," said the director. "You will receive ten lashes."

Akim looked at him without saying anything.

"I'm annoyed, Alexander Akim, as annoyed as I could possibly be," he went on, drawing closer to him. "Why have you made it necessary for me to take such a measure? Who advised you to run away like that? Weren't you going to be free? Think of that girl who's been waiting for you since yesterday."

Akim still had his eyes fixed on him.

"Well," continued the irritated director, "after the punishment we'll try to forget all about it. I wish you good luck. The overseer is coming."

As usual, the punishment took place in the shed. Akim drank a glass of alcohol and the overseer, according to custom, asked his forgiveness, but with a sincerity and sadness that were out of the ordinary. The other prisoners, frightened at being treated to an execution rather than a party, were mute and stunned. After the first blow, Akim lost consciousness; but, with the third he came back to his senses and suffered a mortal pain. Between each blow, he had to wait while the overseer recovered his strength; he didn't know if he would live long enough to be killed by another blow; he was torn apart, humiliated, menaced by the thought of staying alive while enduring an agony powerful enough to kill him. At the sixth blow he heard the trumpets at the head of the procession announcing the celebration. The prisoners, suddenly inspired by these rejoicings which they so desperately wanted, urged him to stick it out. The overseer hastened to finish the ordeal. Akim was still alive when he fell from the torturer's hands.

The director himself led Elise to her fiancé's bedside. She was not pretty and she was crying. Nevertheless, he gave her a sort of smile, but his swollen lips, his half-open eyes, and slashed cheeks turned it into a horribly cynical expression.

"Well, that's it, it's finished," the director said. "I'm glad to see that everything turned out for the best. There's really no reason to talk about it again."

The orderly was not allowed to take care of prisoners after punishments. They helped each other awkwardly, with a special repugnance for everything that had to do with wounds and sores.

"Does it hurt?" the director asked stupidly. He looked at the stranger's black eyes that were stubbornly fixed on him, the bloodied mouth, the hands clammy with sweat.

"Say something to him"—he leaned towards Elise and pushed her forward—"tell him you're not bitter about what he did."

But the sobbing girl drew back, frightened.

"Still, someone has to try to help him," he added, upset by those stubborn black eyes that did not stop looking at him. "Doesn't he want to talk?"

Piotl came in, followed by his family, even though this was against the rules.

"If he goes to sleep," he said, "that's the end."

"Perhaps there are death rites in his country," the director said. "It looks as though he's waiting. Didn't he ever talk to one of you about it?"

"Death is death," said the old man. "Leave him alone."

The footsteps of the guests could be heard around the shed. The people had been stirred up by the change in plans—but they were also upset, and they walked around without saying anything. Louise came in and took Elise by the arm.

"This is no place for a young girl," she said. "Come outside with me to wait for the news."

But the girl, her face blinded by tears, escaped from her and snuggled up beside the old man.

"What does he want, then?" asked the director, looking at those large brilliant eyes, those extraordinarily large and pure eyes that were still fixed on him.

"He wants to die," said Piotl. "Believe me, nothing more."

After the ordeal the overseer had fallen into a state of exhaustion akin to sleep; now he woke from his spell and began to groan.

"Please be quiet," the director said, glad to be able to turn his head away. "Someone keep that brute quiet."

"Watch," said the old man, "something's going to happen. He's moving."

Louise again took the girl by the arm.

"Come out with me," she said. "We'll come back in a moment."

The girl went off without protest.

"Do you want something?" the director asked. "Can I help you? Won't you let me know what you want?"

The eyes kept looking at him, but they were becoming cloudy: one of his hands rose slightly.

"How terrible!" sighed the director. "Can't we know what he

wants?"

"Be quiet," the old man said gruffly. "Right now, he doesn't want anything at all. He's going to sleep."

The men began to make signs, to remove their hats, to wipe their faces.

"Yes," said the director, "it's the end."

He waited several moments, examined the quivering face, and then, after staunching the wounds with his handerchief, gently closed the eyes that could no longer see.

"You're losing a good comrade," he said to the others. "I'm sorry, truly sorry."

A large bier was set up in the entryway, and the guests remained to attend the funeral. The sun was shining now with a lovely radiance. The flowers in the garden, still a little wet, opened up. Branches came through the windows and tossed gently in the rooms.

"My dear," Louise said to the girl, who was sobbing on the bench with her head in her hands, "don't cry like that, my dear."

She drummed her fingers mechanically on her knees. Then, looking at the superb and victorious sky, the sky that in spite of death and tears still bound her under the mirror of spring to the reflections of an unshakeable faith, she rose to attend to her duties as mistress of the house.

the last word

The words I heard that day rang strangely in my ears. I hailed a stranger on the finest street in the city.

"Can you tell me what the watchword is?"

"I'd be happy to tell you," he answered, "but somehow I haven't managed to hear it yet today."

"Never mind," I said. "I'll go find Sophonie."

He gave me a dark look.

"I'm not too happy with your language. Are you sure of your words?"

"No," I said, shrugging my shoulders. "How can I be sure? That's the risk you run."

I walked towards the esplanade; on the way I passed a narrow lane and heard sounds coming from a loudspeaker. A woman came out onto a porch.

"You're not ugly," she said, after looking me over. "But just now I can't ask you in. Imagine, a day like this!" The esplanade was at the edge of the city. As always, the sun was bathing it in a true light. Some children were playing on a pile of sand, but as soon as they saw me they started squawking hideously. They threw stones at me to block my way.

"May I go to the library?" I asked the janitor, entering a majestic building guarded by two bronze lions.

"What?" asked the janitor, with a frightened expression. "Will you be the last one? Go up quickly, time's running out."

I went into an enormous room. The walls were covered with empty shelves.

"I've come late," I said to a dry little man who was pacing back and forth. "What should I do?"

"Be quiet," he answered harshly. "This is the hour of solitude," and then he pushed me into a cell and carefully closed the door.

There was a book lying open on the table, apparently put there for me. Thinking I was alone, I was about to take a look at it when an old woman sleeping on some blankets in the corner let out a cry.

"I didn't see you," I said. "Does my presence disturb you?"

"Not at all. But at my age, I'm not used to visitor."

I sat down beside her. Then, with my eyes closed, I began to go through the customary greetings: "I didn't know you. I sought in vain to approach your face. Everything that is beautiful about you lies in the foul depths whose image I was pursuing. I called out to you, and your name was the echo of my basest thoughts. Days of shame. Now it's too late. I stand before you to offer up the spectacle of my mistakes."

"Come close, then," said the old woman. "We'll spend these few moments together."

She took off her clothes. Her body was covered in long black tights. She went over to get the book and then tore out some pages. She handed me a few of them; we sat down side by side, each wrapped in a blanket.

"This is an excerpt from the discourse on the third State," I said to her, after looking at the pages. "Listen to what it says. 'There was a time when language no longer linked words according to simple relationships. It became such a delicate instrument that most people were forbidden to use it. But men naturally lack wisdom. The desire to be united through outlawed bonds never left them in peace, and they mocked this decree. In the face of such folly, reasonable people decided to stop speaking. Those who had not been forbidden to speak, who knew how to express themselves, resolved to stay silent from then on. They seemed to have learned words only to forget them. Associating them with what was most secret, they turned them away from their natural course.' "

"I have only a few lines to read," the woman said when her turn came. But after beginning to spell out the word shipwreck in a very clumsy way, she added: "Excuse me, I can't go on."

She quickly got dressed again. Rummaging through one of her pockets, she took out a picture of a child's head.

"Accept this token. I have nothing else to give you to make up for the wrong I've done you."

"What do you mean?" I muttered. "What are you doing?"

Once again she leaned over the page that she had let drop to the floor.

"These things are not for people my age," she declared. "I'm sorry to have caused trouble for you, but I can't fulfill my role."

"I'm sorry. It's late now, and I'm going to sleep."

I fell into a sound sleep, but I was soon woken up again. "This won't do," I said. I pounced on the book. I wanted to tear it apart, to bite it. "Why am I being humiliated like this? What should I do? What have I forgotten?" Once again, I fell asleep. As I slept, the walls of the cell became covered with a brownish color. A dry vegetation similar to lichen overran the floor. A bitch crawled under the table, followed by her puppies, and I knew that she was howling weakly, ferociously: nothing could have been more hideous.

"What a racket!" I muttered in my sleep.

The cell had a round window made of opaque glass that resembled a porthole. Someone was pushing on it from the outside. Heavy pieces of plaster, eaten away by dampness, fell on the floor, exposing crumbling bricks in the walls. A thick vapor entered through the window, as though some mouth were spewing it out in fitful gusts. The woman shook me: "We have to read again," she said in an anguished voice. I pressed my face against the ground and said with the stubborness of sleep:

"You can't see what I see."

"Well," said the old woman. "I'll make you a more comfortable bed." She pushed me into a corner and then threw several blankets there as well.

A black cloud with coppery reflections had gathered on the ceiling. A veil of darkness fell from this cloud, then a plume of sparks that swept the air. Excited by these lights, the dogs began to prowl through the room—and then they suddenly jumped at me. I hid under the covers, but they knew where I was, and one by one they took little bites out of my neck.

"What a bad night," I shouted, throwing off the blankets. I tried to get some rest, but to no avail. Then an idea occurred to me: Why was this book so different from the others?

At that moment the door opened. Shouting and singing came from the esplanade, all the noises of a crowd about to take part in an event. "It's time to go," the old woman said. "The procession is waiting. We're the last ones." I got up quickly and walked through the library, where I went and knocked on a large glass door.

"I'm entitled to some explanation," I said to the librarian, who was arranging miniscule objects on a table. "Why wasn't I told the watchword?"

"Because there is no watchword anymore," he said, without looking up. Then he showed me some objects that appeared to have been carved from the finest ivory. They were the smallest figures I had ever seen. "What do you think of these curios?" They reminded me of the animals who had been harrassing me in my sleep.

"You can't get rid of me like that," I shouted. "How am I

supposed to live now? Who will I talk to?"

After speaking these words I had to leave the room and go out into the street. I saw the old woman in front of the large door. She was looking at me with a malicious smile: "Have you heard the news? There's no more library. From now on, people can read any way they like." "I want to kill you," I said to her, grabbing hold of her arm.

I walked with her from street to street, right into the middle of a chaotic celebration, with torches burning in broad daylight. A tremendous din of shouting rose up in response to an underground command, and it carried the whole crowd as one, back and forth from east to west. At some intersections the earth trembled, and it seemed that the people were walking over the void, crossing it on a footbridge of cries. The great consecration of *until* took place around noon. Using only little scraps of words, as if all that remained of language were the forms of a long sentence crushed by the crowd's trampling feet, they sang the song of a single word that could still be made out, no matter how loud the shouting. This word was *until*. "Listen," said the one who had been chosen to give the speech, "I beg you to pay attention to your words. When you say, *I will love you until the day you are unfaithful to me*, listen carefully. What have you said? You must be like a boat that has a rudder and in spite of that never manages to reach the shore. Through the intermediary of *until*, time throws back the rocks and becomes its own wreckage."

The people went home. The loudspeaker on the main street said to the crowd: "Don't neglect your worries." "I live far away," I said to the old woman, "and you might be pressed for time. Don't feel obligated to go with me." But she stayed with me everywhere. When we came to my house, she opened the door and forced me to enter a long hallway that went down into the ground. Being in this cellar made me short of breath, and I begged her to take me back outside.

"Where are we going?" I asked her. "What am I going to find now? I'm no more than an intruder in my own house. Can you explain to me what all this is about?"

But the woman was still completely absorbed by the celebration. She could think only of reminding me of the sudden changes that had taken place.

"I don't understand what you're worried about," she said. "Didn't you feel how good life can still be here during the procession? As we were walking down the streets, I took off my shoes and let myself be carried along by the crowd. It was pressing all around me. The cries came from a very deep place, they went through my body and came out of my mouth. I spoke without having to say a word."

"Enough of your blathering," I shouted. "I need to be alone."

She took the elevator upstairs and left me with my face against the ground. "O city," I prayed, "since the time is coming when I will no longer be able to communicate with you in my own language, allow me to rejoice to the end in the things that words correspond to when they break apart." A joyful clapping of hands called me upstairs, where I found the table set.

"Make the introductions," the woman said to me. She pointed to a corner where a young woman was sitting with a thick bandage around her neck.

"I don't know anyone here," I said, sitting down at the table. "Don't ask me to do it."

Everyone ate heartily, but at the end of the meal the thing I had been dreading happened: the girl threw herself at my knees and sobbed: "I beg of you, please recognize me." I stood up. She put her hand to her throat and undid the bandage. Ah! What have I seen! "World of mud," I thought, "where even dreams deceive you."

I ran away. It was already dusk. The city was invaded by

smoke and clouds. Only the doors of the houses were visible, barred with gigantic inscriptions. A cold dampness was shining on the cobblestones. When I went down the stairway beside the river, some large dogs appeared on the opposite bank. They were similar to mastiffs and their heads bristled with crowns of thorns. I knew that the justice department used these dogs from time to time and that they had been trained to be quite ferocious. But I belonged to the justice department as well. That was my shame: I was a judge. Who could condemn me? Instead of filling the night with their barking, the dogs silently let me pass, as though they had not seen me. It was only after I had walked some distance that they began to howl again: trembling, muffled howls, which at that hour of the day resounded like the echo of the words *there is*.

"Those are probably the last words," I thought, listening to them.

But the words *there is* were still able to reveal the things that were in this remote neighborhood. Before reaching the pavillion, I entered a real garden with trees, roots tangled along the ground, a whole forest of branches and plants. The youngest children in the city were shut up in this pavillion—the ones who could talk only with shouts and cries. As soon as I went in, I was addressed by a very disagreeable looking woman:

"You have insulted my sons. What do you have to say in your defense?"

This woman was closed in between two halves of a table and did not have the freedom to do anything but stand up.

"Where are they?" I asked, trying to get away.

"No funny business! And don't go upstairs. It's a holiday today."

Upstairs, the children were noisily playing ball in a wide-open classroom. When I entered, everyone became silent. Each child went to his place quietly, and, as the veil fell over the statue of the teacher, their heads lined up hypocritically on their desks. I stood in front of a small table beside the plaster statue and indicated that it was time for work to begin. Right away, they asked me the traditional question that is asked in schools: "Are you the teacher or God?" I looked at them sadly. There were so many ways to answer them, but first I had to bring order to the class.

"Listen," I said to them, "at this special hour, we can help each other. I, too, am a little child in a cradle, and I need to speak with cries and tears. Let's be friends."

A lively child, older than the others, was sent to me by a delegation. He had red hair.

"Be reasonable," I said, holding out my hand to him. "It's in both our interests to see if we speak the same language. But first, you have to learn the alphabet."

I wrote out several sentences on the blackboard. For example: *Fear is your only master. If you think you are no longer afraid of anything, reading is useless. But it is the lump of fear in your throat that will teach you how to speak*. Then I alluded to my own torments.

"What happens when you live inside books for too long? You forget the first word and the last word."

"One moment," the boy shouted to me. "What is your connection to the statue?"

"So you're logicians, like everyone else. But first you must take my sadness into account. It wasn't just anyone you threw those stones at on the esplanade. I'm more vulnerable than other people, since no one can condemn me."

"Okay," said the child. "Let's move on to the commentary."

He went over to the pedestal of the statue and took out a large, thickly bound book. He opened it to a page marked with a red line. This text obliged me to give them a serious warning:

"Since the watchword was done away with," I said, "reading

is free. If you think I talk without knowing what I'm saying, you are within your rights. I'm only one voice among many."

I couldn't stop trembling. I read the sentences and broke up their meaning by replacing some of the words with gasps and sighs. After a few moments the clamoring of the pupils merged with my groans, and I wrote out the passage on the blackboard, so that everyone could become familiar with it. *When the census of the population was taken, it happened that an individual by the name of Thomas was not included in the general list. He therefore became superfluous, and others began treating him as if, in relation to humanity—which was itself insane—he had lost his mind.* Then, according to custom, I asked the youngest child to pronounce each word along with me as loudly as he could. This attempt showed the enormous difference between a mature man and a child. Another passage from the same work was juxtaposed with the first to demonstrate the analogies of meaning. It included the last lines of the fable about the beseiged one: *The storm ended at the moment when the enemies took the balloon of the only surviving inhabitant and sent it off into the air. How did he manage to get away? By what means did he trick the guards and leave a place that was hemmed in on all sides? No one could say, and not even he knew how it was done.*

"What I suggest," I said, "is to cross out all these words and replace them with the word *not*. For this is my commentary: after his extraordinary escape, no sooner did the inhabitant of the city set foot on free ground than he discovered the walls of his enormous prison all around him. He is asked: how was he able to get over the ramparts and fly through the air? But he doesn't know, and he can only express what has happened to him by saying: nothing happened."

The children all stood up at a single bound. They gathered around the statue, the oldest ones touching the robe, striking it as if it were made of brass or bronze and could strike them back.

But this ceremony soon wearied them. Abandoning their reserve, they threw themselves on their visitor, screaming and showering him with displays of affection; some climbed up on the table, others pulled the chair from behind and tried to make it tip over; still others struggled to pull off pieces of my clothing. All this, of course, took place without a word. Finally, a person the children themselves looked upon with dread—and whom they had been hiding behind them until now—emerged from under the benches and came face to face with the teacher. He was extremely handsome, but an abundant outpouring of saliva kept falling from his mouth and soaking his clothes. Through the river that was flowing down his chin, this young person began to reprimand the teacher who had spoken too much, attacking him in the name of some former ideal of language. But I saw that this watery mouth was also trying to make itself understood. In order to reduce it to silence, he abruptly had to give up centuries of pride and return it to a state of innocence that the quest for the first word would not disturb, and it occurred to me that this spittle was the prophecy of a universal unhappiness. I became afraid, stood up, and stepped back among all those children who were gathered around me. They began to hiss like vipers, to sway from side to side and back and forth in a regular motion. I grabbed a piece of chalk and on the blackboard drew the face of the young mute—emerging from the mouth of a volcano amidst a shower of stones, rays of light, and garbage of every kind.

"This is our judge," I cried out. "In the name of what will you judge us? Who will challenge you? Poor children. A wound like this is caused by language, and it imposes no restraints on you."

The hissing and whistling pierced the air and became so strident that the whole house was shaken and a sheet of ice fell between the teacher and his pupils. I saw them through this frozen water, and at each deeper level it reflected shadows that became more and more jumbled. I saw myself in these images, and they were taking me back to childhood. At the bottom of this ocean, the door opened and the mother began to scream: "Give me back my sons!" The only thing I could do was leave, but before going I made this statement:

"The pupil listens to the teacher with docility. He learns his lessons from him and loves him. He makes progress. But if one day he sees this teacher as God, then he ridicules him and no longer knows anything."

The sound of their jeering accompanied me to the garden. There, I fell down. The saddest rays of the evening were at that moment reaching the city: houses in ruin, black trees painted against the sky. The great eagle with red wings that was set loose at dusk to drive back the threat of night now mingled with the shadows he was supposed to chase away, and I could hear his anxious cry through the fog that seemed to have become an immense nocturnal bird. I stood up and ran along the road that went down to where the arenas had been carved out of the rock. It was a desert, and drunken women sometimes walked there. The sound of footsteps aroused unknown animals from the city, and you moved toward the end of the territory through a whirl of insects, flies, and half-blind beasts. At that hour of the night, the mountain was empty.

"Where are you going?" shouted a woman, who was lying on the slope.

"To the tower!"

But several steps later, I bumped against a body and stopped. The girl I had knocked into emerged slowly from sleep and looked at me without saying anything. Because she was drunk, she saw me as I was.

"Are you the judge, then?" she asked with an expression of great surprise.

"Yes," I said, "but I can only judge myself."

She threw herself at my knees and muttered: "Rescue me

from this wine I've drunk"—"All right! Let's run together," and then, taking her by the arm, I dragged her along with me. At a crossroads, the path came to an end.

"There's nothing here," I said. "Do you want me to take off your coat?"

It was a heavy robe made of gold cloth and it was trailing along the ground. She folded it over her arm and looked at me provocatively. "You see," she said, "I'm naked." But this veiled nakedness was not the sort of nakedness that called for the axe.

"Even at the point of death," I said, "a judge can't marry a guilty person without some minimal ceremony."

"Yes," she murmured, "but the evening is so black."

It was true that the darkness seemed to be carrying flowers for a festival. At the top of the hills, the animals that had been looking for shelter were all cries and complaints. I opened the material she was wrapped up in and got inside with her. For a few moments I became a man from another city. After that, she made this confession to me: "Drunkenness doesn't help me at all."—"Take a look at yourself, then," I said to her. She opened her coat a little and saw red spots all over her body, like marks of fire.

"Let's run now. I've drunk too much wine also."

Before reaching the tower, we had to walk across a vast plain that was covered with rocks and large stones. The expanse was so empty that we hesitated as we tried to find our way, even though the huge structure was only a few steps in front of us.

"It's my turn to confide in you now. I've condemned myself, it's true. I can't bear to talk without knowing what I'm saying."

"Strange language. To hear you talk, you'd think you were already a new man."

"Your insults won't change anything. You were in my path, and now you have to stay with me until the end."

"Let's keep going. We'll continue walking together."

After skirting some enormous rocks, we came to an enclosure surrounded by a large wall. "Whose guest are you going to be?" she asked me, suddenly worried. I pointed to the top of the tower and dragged her inside. We climbed the staircase very slowly; it seemed to take up the whole width of the structure. Half-way to the top, a memory came back to me. "Poor mute girl," I thought. "Here is where my scruples come to an end." We kept climbing: through an opening I saw how high above the countryside we already were. The nakedness of the desert absorbed the stones that were piled up around it, and the holes dug in the sand opened surprising paths that showed how deep the ground was. Several steps from the top, I became dizzy, and images of the city we had left behind passed before my eyes.

"Stay here," I told her.

I entered a small room that turned the tower into a lookout post. From there, the view extended all the way to the esplanade, where you could see bodies laid out on stretchers; it was the hour closest to night; these unfortunate and tormented people were suffering from what they thought was a cure, and they were crushed by the shame that had thrown them into the arms of a savior. You could see through it to the outside, and at the same time it reflected the things within. Right away, I had a severe attack. What an attack! It seemed to me that I was holding a gigantic, sleeping body in my arms—its weight, smell, and warm dampness proved that it came from some foul place. I couldn't put it on the floor. But I could hardly let it decompose on my lap either. My body shook, and the images of the room I could still see broke into pieces. Everything burst, tore apart, came from the depths. I was choking. I felt that I was hanging from the top of a tower that had already fallen—only to be rebuilt by my hatred of mankind. I myself flew into fragments, and yet I was unhurt. I cried out. I called to the girl, "My body is burning up." She opened her coat a little and showed me the marks of fire. They seemed to be forming the first shapes of a vague language.

I opened my eyes on this white body and sent her away. By looking in the mirror I was better able to see how the rock piles had fallen into their present shapes—and how they preserved the memory of the past. Everywhere in front of me there had once been splendid structures, and the heavy stability of the stones recalled those buildings that had now collapsed. I took several steps in the room. The only things in it were a chair and a rope for ringing the bell at the top of the tower. Timidly, I opened the door a crack and looked out at the darkness.

"Let me in," said the girl, who was waiting. "It's completely dark out here."

But even though the room was also without light, a weak phosphorescence came in from the outside, and she screamed and covered her eyes.

"Yes," I said, "you see it too—this terrible sun that burns and casts no light."

And I fell back into my lugubrious storm. The distant constellations rose in the sky. Thanks to the patience of my inert, almost paralyzed gaze, I was able to follow them, slow as they were. I broke the window, my hands were cut, my blood flowed drop by drop through this hole into the sky. It seemed to me that my eyes were finally closed. They were burning me, I couldn't see a thing; they were consuming me, and this burning gave me the happiness of being blind. Death, I thought. But then, something terrible happened. At the core of my sightless eyes the sky opened up, and it saw everything, and the vestige of the smoke and tears that had obscured them rose up to infinity, where it dissipated in light and glory. I began to stammer.

"What do you mean?" the girl shouted. She slapped me in the face. "Why do you have to speak?"

"I must explain things clearly to you," I said. "Up to the last moment, I'm going to be tempted to add one word to what has been said. But why would one word be the last? The last word is no longer a word, and yet it is not the beginning of anything else. I ask you to remember this, so you'll understand what you're seeing: the last word cannot be a word, nor the absence of words, nor anything else but a word. If I break apart because I stammer, I'll have to pay for it in my sleep, I'll wake up and then everything will begin again."

"Why so many precautions?"

"You know very well—there's no more watchword. I have to take on everything myself."

"Farewell, then," and she held out her hand to me, then withdrew to the back of the room.

I reached into my pocket, took out a photograph of a child that had been given to me by a woman I had met, and put it on the wall at eye-level. The picture immediately burst apart; it scorched my eyes and tore out a section of the wall. But this hole, opening on the emptiness again, didn't show me anything: it closed off my view, and the freer the horizon appeared to be, the more this freedom became a power to see nothing the emptiness would give in to. No eye could be reborn from such an exchange—it was as slight as the beating of a butterfly's wings. I turned to stone. I was the monument and the hammer that breaks it. I collapsed to the ground. I was still lying there when I received a visit from the owner of the tower.

"What's this?" he said to me. "What games are you playing here? There are customs and rituals when people come to my house. And who is this woman?"

I struggled to my feet and said in a low voice: "You see, you don't know anything." But I was so weak that I had to sit down, and the man put the bell-rope around my neck.

"I'm going to tell you about this building—which you seem to have entered in order to amuse yourself. It is the last tower left.

It must not fall into ruin like the others. Spend some time here, if you like, but give up the hope of seeing it collapse on top of you at the last moment."

I felt the chill that came from these words.

"You're the owner of the tower," I muttered. "It's natural for you to think it's indestructible and that it won't fall down. But I don't own anything."

"If you can hold out until the cock crows," he said, raising his voice, "you will see that I am the All Powerful One."

I laughed at these words, but this laughter robbed me of my last strength. How could I be so weak and yet still be able to talk? What weakness! What weariness! I knew that I was already too weak to die, and I saw myself as I was—an unlucky man who has no life and yet who struggles to live. It was this weakness that the master of the place was trying to take advantage of. What did he want from me? He made fun of my dizziness, he appeared and disappeared, he shouted: "Look me in the face," and also: "Who can deny me?" and also, quite suddenly, with a strange voice, the softest, most soothing voice I had ever heard: "My accomplice." What a voice! "Is it possible?" I said to myself, standing up. And then, what happened? I loved him, too, and in loving him I defied him. I bowed down, I humbled myself before him as though before a sovereign; and because I treated him as master, I chained him to his sovereignty. And we were bound together in such a way that for him to become who he was again, he had to say to me: "I'm laughing at you because I'm no more than a beast," but with that confession my adoration became twice as great, and in the end there was nothing left but a sad animal, watched over by a servant who swatted away the flies. A ray of sunlight, erect like a stone, enclosed both of them in an illusion of eternity. They blissfully sank into repose.

The woman, beside herself with worry, came over to wake them.

"Get up," she cried. "The woods are on fire and the earth is shaking."

She got down on her knees and begged them to save her.

"A woman's illusion," said the owner. "Everything is peaceful. The night beats in vain against the walls of the city."

"Help," she cried again, shaking them both. "Water is flooding the countryside, there's a storm blowing in the desert."

But they both looked at her skeptically. At that moment, through the window with the broken pane, they could hear cries of distress from an enormous crowd.

"We're lost," the woman said. "The city is in darkness. Better to run away than to stay in this tottering old building."

"Make her be silent," the owner said to his companion. "Her shouting is spoiling my sleep."

She tried to open the door, but a horrible noise shook the tower. "The staircase is collapsing," she shouted. Irritated, the master of the house took her in his hands. "I've ruled over the world," he scolded, "it shouldn't be difficult for me to make you be quiet." During this time, flames began to light up the room. "Come, come, don't be so nervous: we'll have no trouble getting along with each other." As a wave of stone and sand struck the building, he held her tightly in his arms.

"Oh no," she said, "can't you feel that we're not standing on anything?"

But he reassured her with his calmness, and when the tower collapsed and threw them outside, all three of them fell without saying a word.

1935, 1936

after the fact

Mallarmé to an unpublished author who had asked him to write an introduction or prefatory note to his work: "I abhor prefaces that come from the author himself, but those that come from someone else I find even more distasteful. My friend, a real book needs no introduction; it's a bolt from the blue, and it behaves like a woman with her lover, needing no help from a third party, the husband . . ."

In a completely different context I have written: "*Noli me legere.*" A prohibition against reading that tells the author he has been disposed of. "You will not read me." "I do not remain as a text to be read except through the process that slowly devours you while writing." "You will never know what you have written, even if you have written only to find this out."

Prior to the work, the work of art, the work of writing, the work of words, there is no artist—neither a writer nor a speaking subject—since it is the production that produces the producer, bringing him to life or making him appear in the act of substantiating him (which, in a simplified manner, is the teaching of Hegel and even the Talmud: doing takes precedence over being, which does not create itself except in creating—what? Perhaps anything: how this anything is judged depends on time, on what happens, on what does not happen: what we call historical factors, history, without however looking to history for the last judgment). But if the written work produces and substantiates the writer, once created it bears witness only to his dissolution, his disappearance, his defection and, to express it more brutally, his death, which itself can never be definitely verified: for it is a death that can never produce any verification.

Thus, before the work, the writer does not yet exist; after the work, he is no longer there: which means that his existence is open to question—and we call him an "author!" It would be more correct to call him an "actor," the ephemeral character who is born and dies each evening in order to make himself extravagantly seen, killed by the performance that makes him visible—that is, without anything of his own or hiding anything in some secret place.

From the "not yet" to the "no longer"—this is the path of what we call the writer, not only his time, which is always suspended, but what brings him to life through an interrupted becoming.

Has anyone noticed that Valéry, in imagining the utopia of Monsieur Teste, was the most romantic of men without knowing it? In his notes he writes innocently: "*Ego*—I dreamed of a being who had the greatest gifts—not to do anything with them, having assured himself [how?] that he had them. I told Mallarmé about it one Sunday on the quai d'Orsay." Now, what is this being—a musician, a philosopher, a writer, an artist, a Sovereign—who *can* do everything and yet does nothing? None other than the romantic genius, an I so superior to itself and its creation that it proudly forbids itself to be shown, a God then who refuses to be a demiurge, the infinite All Powerful One who will not condescend to be limited by a work, no matter how sublime (cf. Duchamp). Or else, it is in the most ordinary things that the extraordinary ones must be felt: no masterpiece (what poverty, what mediocrity in this master; to accept nothing less than being the greatest, the highest); but if Teste betrays himself, it is through the mystery of banality, through what makes him *appear* as someone unperceived. (I do not intend to diminish Valéry by revealing the adolescent naiveté of his central project, and even less so because on top of this there is the demand of extreme modesty: the "genius" can only hide himself, efface himself; he cannot leave behind any marks, cannot do anything that could show him to be superior in what he does and even in what he is; the divine incognito, the hidden God, who does not hide himself in order to make the one who finally finds him more praiseworthy, but because he is ashamed of being God or knowing himself to be God—or, furthermore, God must remain unknown to himself, or else we would give him a Self, a self in our own image. I don't know if Freud, the unbeliever, thought that he had made the unconscious his God.)

After this parenthesis, I return to the problem. If the written word, which is always impersonal, changes, dismisses, and abolishes the writer as writer, if not the man or the writing subject (others will say that it enriches him, that it makes him more than he was before, that he is created by it—from which comes the traditional notion of the author—or else that it has no other end except to allow him to use his mind—Valéry again), yes, if the work, in its operation, no matter how slight it is, is so destructive as to engage the operator in the equivalent of suicide, then how can he turn back (ah, the guilty Orpheus) to what he believes he is leading into the light—to judge it, to consider it, to recognize himself in it and, in the end, to make himself the privileged reader of it, the principle commentator or simply the zealous helper who gives or imposes his version, resolves the enigma, reveals the secret and authoritatively interrupts (we are, after all, talking about the author) the hermeneutic chain, since he claims to be the adequate interpreter, the first or the last?

Noli me legere. Does this impossibility have an aesthetic, ethical, or ontological value? We would have to look at it more closely. It is a polite appeal, a strange warning, a prohibition that has always let itself be violated already. "Please do not. . ." If the work is comparable to Eurydice, the request—the very humble request—not to turn around to look at it (or to read it) is just as anguishing for it, the one who knows that the "law" will make it disappear (or at least illuminate it to such a degree that it will dissolve in the light) that it is a temptation for the enchanter whose whole desire is to persuade himself that there is someone beautiful following him, rather than a futile simulacrum or a void wrapped in vain words. Even Mallarmé, the most secretive and discrete of poets, gives some hints as to the manner in which the *Coup de dés* should be read. Even Kafka read his stories to his sisters, sometimes even to a public audience, which, finally, does not mean that he read them for himself as pieces of writing—an affirmation of writing—but dangerously agreed to lend them his voice, to substitute for the legend (the enigma of what must be read) the living and speaking evidence of a diction and a presence that imposed its own meaning—or at least a meaning.

Such a temptation is necessary. To give in to it is perhaps inevitable. I remember the story, *Madame Edwarda*. I was surely one of the first to read it and to be convinced (overwhelmed to the point of silence) of what was unique about this work (only several pages long) and what set it above all literature, and in such a way that there could never be any word of commentary attached to it. I exchanged a few emotional words with Georges Bataille, not in the way you talk to an author about a book of his you admire, but in order to make him understand that such an encounter was enough for my entire life, just as the fact of having written the book should have been enough for his. All this happened during the worst days of the Occupation. This small book—the most minimal of books, published under a pseudonym and read by just a few people—was destined to sink clandestinely into the probable ruin of each of us (author, reader)—with no traces left of this remarkable event. As we know, things turned out differently.

Even so, without overstepping the bounds of tact, I would like to add something. Later, when the war was over and Georges Bataille's life had also changed, he was asked to republish the book—or, more accurately, to allow it to be given a real publication. To my great horror, he told me one day that he wanted to write a sequel to *Madame Edwarda* and asked my advice. I felt as though someone had just punched me; I blurted out: "It's impossible. I beg of you, don't touch it." The matter was then dropped, at least between the two of us. It will be remembered that he could not prevent himself from writing a preface under his own name, chiefly to introduce his name, so that he could take responsibility (indirectly) for a piece of writing that was still considered scandalous. But this preface, no matter how important it was, did not in the least undermine the absolute nature of *Madame Edwarda*—nor have the full- scale commentaries it has inspired (particularly the one by Lucette Finas and, more recenlty, the one by Pierre-Phillipe Jandin). All that can be said, all that I can say myself, is that the reading of this book has probably changed. Admiration, reflection, comparison with other works—the things that perpetuate a book are the very things that flatten it or equalize it; if the book raises up literature, literature reduces it to its own level, no matter what importance we might give it. What remains is the nakedness of the word "writing," a word no less powerful than the feverish revelation of what for one night, and forever after that, was "Madame Edwarda."

Vicious Circles. I have been asked—someone inside me has asked—to communicate with myself, as a way of introducing these two old stories, so old (nearly fifty years old) that, without even taking into account the difficulties I have just expressed, it is not possible for me to know who wrote them, how they were written, and to what unknown urgency they were responding. I remember (it is only a memory and perhaps false) that I was astonishingly cut off from the literature of the time and knew about nothing except what is called classical literature, with nevertheless some inkling of Valéry, Göethe, and Jean-Paul. Nothing that could have prepared me to write these innocent stories that resound with murderous echoes of the future. There have been commentaries, profound commentaries that I will take care not to comment on myself, about "The Last Word" (1935). This piece was not written for publication. Nevertheless, it did finally appear twelve years later in the series "L'age d'or" edited by Henri Parisot. But, as it happened, this was the last work in the series—which had run out of funds and was about to disappear—and the book was not even sold anywhere (if I am not mistaken). This was a way of remaining faithful to the title. Undoubtedly, to begin writing only to come so quickly to the end (which was the encounter with the last word), meant at least that there was the hope of not making a career, of finding the quickest way to have done with it right at the start (it would be dishonest to forget that, at the same time or in the meantime, I was writing *Thomas the Obscure*, which was perhaps about the same thing, but precisely did not have done with it and, on the contrary, encountered in the search for annihilation (absence) the impossibility of escaping being (presence)—which was not even a contradiction in fact, but the demand of an endlessness that is unhappy even in dying). In this sense, the story was an attempt to short circuit the other book that was being written, in order to overcome that endlessness and reach a silent decision, reach it through a more linear narrative that was nevertheless painfully complex: which is perhaps why (I don't know) there is the sudden convocation of language, the strange resolution to deprive language of its support, the *watchword* (no more restraining or affirmative language, that is to say, no more language—but no: there is still a speech with which to say this and not to say this), the renunciation of the roles of Teacher and Judge—a renunciation that is itself futile—, the Apocalypse finally, the discovery of nothing other than universal ruin, which is completed with the fall of the last Tower, which is no doubt the Tower of Babel, while at the same time the owner is silently thrown outside (the being who has always assured himself of the meaning of the word "own"—apparently God, even though he is a beast), the narrator who has maintained the privilege of the ego, and the simple and marvelous girl, who probably knows everything, in the humblest kind of way.

This kind of synopsis or outline—the paradox of such a story—is chiefly distinguished by recounting the absolute disaster as having taken place, so that the story itself could not have survived either, which makes it impossible or absurd, unless it claims to be a prophetic work, announcing to the past a future that has already arrived or saying what there still is when there is nothing: *there is*, which holds nothingness and blocks annihilation so that it cannot escape its interminable process whose end is repetition and eternity—the vicious circle.

Prophetic also, but for me (today) in a way that is even more inexplicable, since I can only interpret it in the light of the events that came afterwards and were not known until much later, in such a way that this later knowledge does not illuminate but withdraws understanding from the story that seems to have been named—by antiphrasis?—"The Idyll," or the torment of the happy idea (1936). The theme that I recognize first of all, because Camus made it "familiar" several years later—that is, made it the opposite of what he meant—is indicated in the first words: "the stranger." Who is the stranger? There is no adequate definition here. He comes from somewhere else. He is well received, but received according to rules he cannot submit to and which in any event put him to the test—take him to death's door. He himself draws the "moral" from this and explains it to one of the newcomers: "You'll learn that in this house it's hard to be a stranger. You'll also learn that it's not easy to stop being one. If you miss your country, every day you'll find more reasons to miss it. But if you manage to forget it and begin to love your new place, you'll be sent home, and then, uprooted once more, you'll begin a new exile." Exile is neither psychological nor ontological. The exile cannot accomodate himself to his condition, nor to renouncing it, nor to turning exile into a mode of residence. The immigrant is tempted to naturalize himself, through marriage for example, but he continues to be a migrant. In a place where there is no way out, to escape is the demand that restores the call of the outside. Is it a vain attempt? The prison is not a prison. The guards have their weaknesses, unless their negligence does not belong to the make-believe freedom that would be a temptation and an illusion. Likewise, the extreme politeness, even sincere cordiality of those who regretfully apply the law, does not resemble the tranquil and inflexible "correction" which, several years later, caught willing slaves in the trap of their false humanity, slaves who were incapable of recognizing the masked barbarity that temporarily allowed them to live in a reassuring order.

And yet it is difficult not to think about all this after the fact. Impossible not to think of the ridiculous work carried out in the concentration camps, where the condemned transported mountains of stones from one spot to another and then back to the starting place—not for the glory of some pyramid, but to destroy work itself, along with the sad workers. This happened at Auschwitz, this happened at the Gulag. Which would tend to show that if the imaginary runs the risk of one day becoming real, it is because it has its own rather strict limits and that it can easily foresee the worst because the worst is always the simplest and it always repeats itself.

But I don't think that "The Idyll" can be interpreted as the reading of an already menacing future. History does not withhold meaning, no more than meaning, which is always ambiguous—plural—can be reduced to its historical realization, even the most tragic and the most enormous. That is because the story does not explain itself. If it is the tension of a secret around which it seems to elaborate itself and which immediately declares itself without being elucidated, it only announces its own movement, which can lay the groundwork for the game of deciphering and interpretation, but it remains a *stranger* to itself. From this, it seems to me, and even though it seems to open up the unhappy possibilities of a life without hope, the story as such remains light, untroubled, and of a clarity that neither weighs down nor obscures the pretension of a hidden or serious meaning. The questioning it would imply, I am told, could, in conjunction with the title, be expressed in different forms, all of them necessarily naive and simplistic: for example, why in such a world is the question of the masters' happiness so important and in the end still unresolved? There are appearances, there are only appearances, and how to believe in them, how to call them anything but what they are? Or, is a society which admits that the most unhappy episodes come from itself—either because of this or in spite of this—at heart idyllic? These are some questions, but they are too general to call forth answers, or not to remain questions in spite of the answers they are given. The story contains them perhaps, but on condition that it not be reduced through them to a content, to anything that can be expressed in any other way.

In all respects, it is an unhappy story. But, precisely, as a story, which says all it has to say in saying it, or, better, which announces itself as the clarity that comes both before and as a condition of the serious or ambiguous meaning it also transcribes, it itself is the idyll, the little idol that is unjust and injurious to the very thing it utters, happy in the misfortune it portends and that it endlessly threatens to turn into a lure. This is the law of the story, its happiness and, because of it, its unhappiness, not because, as Valéry reproached Pascal, a beautiful form would necessarily destroy the horror of every tragic truth and make it bearable, even delicious (catharsis). But, before all distinctions between form and content, between signifier and signified, even before the division between utterance and the uttered, there is the unqualifiable Saying, the glory of a "narrative voice" that speaks clearly, without ever being obscured by the opacity or the enigma or the terrible horror of what it communicates.

That is why, in my opinion—and in a way different from the one that led Adorno to decide with absolute correctness—I will say there can be no fiction-story about Auschwitz (I am alluding to *Sophie's Choice*). The need to bear witness is the obligation of a testimony that can only be given—and given only in the singularity of each individual—by the impossible witnesses—the witnesses of the impossible—; some have survived, but their survival is no longer life, it is the break from living affirmation, the attestation that the good that is life (not narcissistic life, but life for others) has undergone the decisive blow that leaves nothing intact. From this it would seem that all narration, even all poetry, has lost the foundation on which another language could be raised—through the extinction of the happiness of speaking that lurks in even the most mediocre silence. Forgetfulness no doubt does its work and allows for works to be made again. But to this forgetfulness, the forgetting of an event in which every possibility was drowned, there is an answer from a failing memory without memories, and the immemorial haunts this memory in vain. Humanity as a whole had to die through the trial of some of its members, (those who incarnate life itself, almost an entire people, a people that has been promised an eternal presence). This death still endures. And from this comes the obligation never again to die only once, without however allowing repetition to inure us to the always essential ending.

I return to "The Idyll," a story from before Auschwitz, a story nevertheless of a wandering that does not end with death and which that death cannot darken, since it ends with the affirmation of the "the superb and victorious sky," a stranger in a strange country, saying that no matter what happens, the light of what is said, even if it is in the unhappiest of words, does not stop shining, in the same way that light and airy radiance always transform the dark night, the night without stars. As if the darkness had become—is this a boon, is this a curse?—yes, had become the shining of the interminable day, the light of the first day.

A story from before Auschwitz. No matter when it is written, every story from now on will be from before Auschwitz. Perhaps life continues. Let us remember the end of *The Metamorphosis*. Right after Gregor Samsa has died in agony and solitude, everything is reborn, and his sister, even though she was the most compassionate of all, gives herself up to the hope of renewal that her young body promises her. Kafka himself thought he threw a shadow on the sun and that once he was gone his family would be happier. So he died, and then what happened? There was only a short time left; almost everyone he loved died in those camps which, no matter what their names, all had the same name: Auschwitz.

I cannot hope for "The Idyll" or "The Last Word" to be read from this perspective (this non-perspective). And yet, even wordless death remains something to be thought about—perhaps endlessly, to the very end. "A voice comes from the other shore. A voice interrupts the words of what has already been said." (Emmanuel Levinas).